SANTA SHARK

BY MIKE LOWERY

Orchard Books

an imprint of Scholastic Inc.

New York

**I**t Was late DECEMBER and SOMEWHERE DEEP DOWN in the OCEAN, STRANGE SOUNDS WERE BUBBLING out of the LITTLE HOUSE that BELONGED to A SHARK NAMED EDGAR.

♪ FA-LA

LOTTA WENT TO INVESTIGATE.

"EDGAR, WHAT ARE YOU DOING AND WHY IS IT SO LOUD?"

SAID THE LITTLE CRAB.

"LOTTA! LONG TIME NO SEA!" SAID EDGAR.

"I'M GLAD YOU'RE HERE. I'M GETTING EVERYTHING READY FOR A VERRRRY SPECIAL GUEST AND I NEED YOUR HELP."

LOTTA TRIED HARD TO GUESS WHO THE SPECIAL GUEST COULD BE.

"IS IT YOUR **AUNT TINA TUNA?**"

"NOPE!" SAID EDGAR. "GUESS AGAIN."

"IS IT **ANTONIO** the *TURTLE?* OR MAYBE OSCAR THE OCTOPUS?"

"**WHO?**" ASKED LOTTA.

EDGAR COULDN'T BELIEVE
THAT HIS BEST FRIEND
(AND THE SMARTEST CRAB IN THE ENTIRE OCEAN)
DIDN'T KNOW WHO HE MEANT.

1 THIS IS SANTA SHARK.

2 HE LIVES AT THE NORTH POLE IN FINLAND.

3 HE HAS A WORKSHOP WHERE HE BUILDS TOYS WITH HIS EELVES!

4 ON CHRISTMAS EVE, KIDS ALL OVER THE WORLD DECORATE THEIR HOMES WITH STUFF LIKE LIGHTS, A TREE WITH A STAR ON TOP, AND FOR SOME REASON, BIG SOCKS.

5 IT STARTS TO **SNOW.**

6 THEN, IT'S **SLEEPY TIME.**

7 SANTA SHARK SWIMS THROUGH THE NIGHT AND SECRETLY DELIVERS GIFTS ON HIS SLEIGH PULLED BY MAGICAL SEAHORSES.

OH! AND WE ALSO HAVE TO PUT OUT A **SNACK.** (SANTA GETS HUNGRY FROM ALL THAT SWIMMING.)

"I DON'T KNOW, EDGAR. THAT STORY IS A LITTLE HARD TO BELIEVE.

"PLUS, HOW CAN WE GET EVERYTHING READY BEFORE BEDTIME?"

YOU KNOW WHAT I ALWAYS SAY...

THEY HUNG LIGHTS.

THEY BAKED TREATS.

THEY DECORATED.

AND SANG CHRISTMAS **CORALS.**

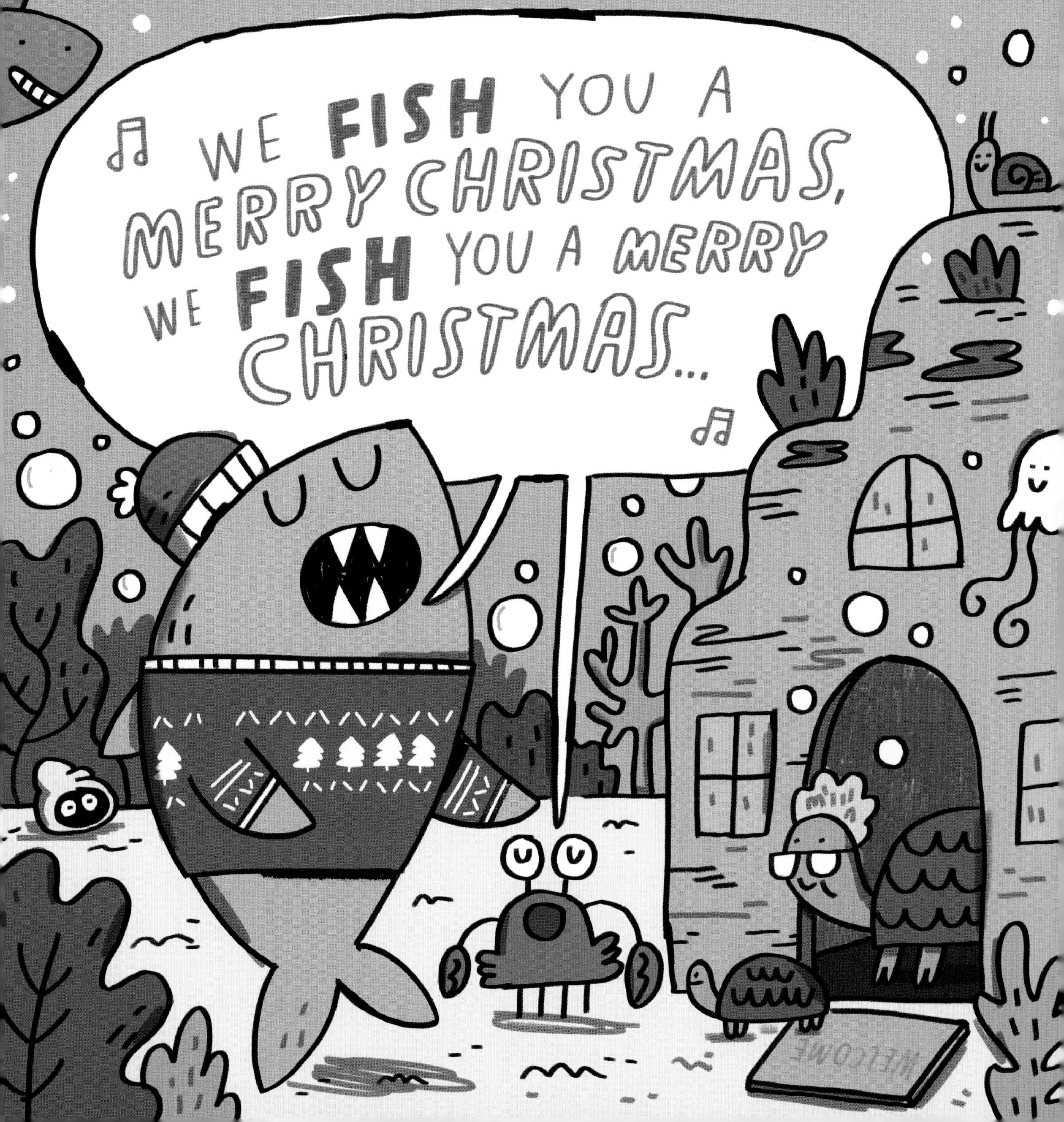

"WHAT ABOUT THE TREE?" ASKED LOTTA.
"I'VE NEVER SEEN ANY IN THE OCEAN."
BUT EDGAR WASN'T WORRIED AT ALL.
HE QUICKLY TRANSFORMED A STALK OF KELP
INTO THE PERFECT SUBSTITUTE.

AND THEY HUNG THE STAR ON TOP TOGETHER.

SOON, IT WAS TIME TO GET READY FOR BED.

EVERYTHING WAS **PERFECT**.

WELL, <u>ALMOST</u> EVERYTHING.

LUCKILY, **LOTTA** HAD AN IDEA.

SHE BORROWED THE **BLOBFISH,**

BLEW LOTS OF **BUBBLES,**

AND **JABBERED** WITH THE JELLYFISH.

SNIFF

AND A FEW MINUTES LATER SHE YELLED,

HEY, EDGAR! COME TAKE A LOOK!

...THE TWO BEST FRIENDS FOUND THE PERFECT CHRISTMAS SURPRISE WAITING FOR THEM UNDER THE TREE.

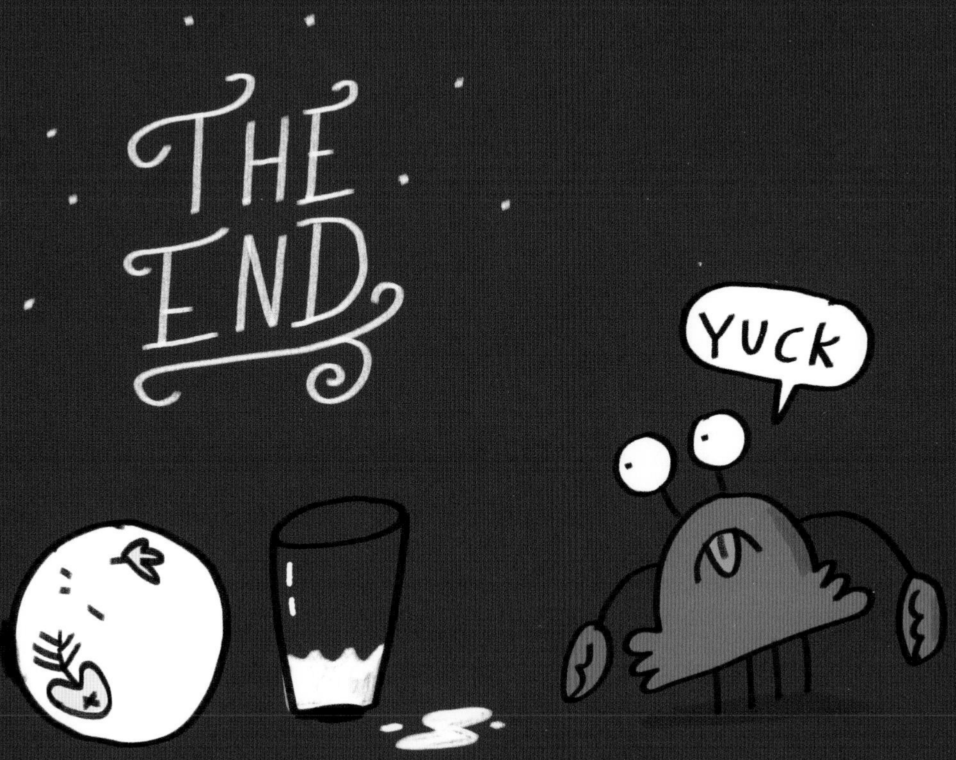
THE END
YUCK

Dedicated to Mom and Dad.
— M.L.

Mike Lowery used to get in trouble for doodling in his books, but now he's doing it for a living. He is the illustrator of many books for kids, including *The Gingerbread Man Loose in the School* and the *New York Times* bestselling Mac B., Kid Spy books. He is also the creator of the Everything Awesome series and Graphix Bug Scout series. He lives in Atlanta with his amazing wife and super-genius kids. He collects weird facts and draws them every day in his sketchbook. See them on Instagram at: @mikelowerystudio.

Library of Congress Cataloging-in-Publication Data available

ISBN 978-1-338-80395-2

10 9 8 7 6 5 4 3 2 1   23 24 25 26 27

Printed in China   38

First edition, October 2023

Book design by Doan Buu and Mike Lowery

The text type and diplay are hand-lettered by Mike Lowery